MW00831142

"What makes debut v
fiction work is the pu
our own reality."

—Wendy J. Fox, Buzzfeed Books

"Jason Teal's *We Were Called Specimens* gives us a new way
to think about and exercise empathy by allowing our whole
selves to participate in his constantly shifting landscape.
We view Marjorie, and we become Marjorie, and the people
we become become Marjorie, so do the people we love.
How do we empathize or heal or love when we are all at once
the grotesque, the horrible, the perpetrator and victim, the hero
and victim? I appreciate Jason Teal's writing for giving
me these large questions."

—Steven Dunn, author of *Potted Meat* and *water & power*

"Jason Teal's debut offering, the courageous and aptly-titled, *We
Were Called Specimens: An Oral Archive of Deity
Marjorie*, successfully breaks free from the detritus, and in
the process, actively distances itself from a cycle of wretched
cookie-cutter assemblage-based musings, (completely) doing
away with cursed meanderings from a self-reflexive past
while sensibly refusing to adopt the American standardised
format of the book. Instead, we are presented with a full and
original discourse on supermodernity, satirical prophecy and
negligible senescence, through a series of carefully inter-
linked meta-vignettes that follow the trajectory of one
Marjorie (a super-deity), as she traverses through a
multitude of (time-spanning) non-linear adventures. The
ideas here are so good, that quite frankly, I believe we are
not going to be seeing anything else quite like it, for a very
long time. It's akin to a sacred text containing the history of
the entire world, as we know it, replete with
masterfully-rendered metaphysical interludes and powerful (but
very real) expressionistic dialogue moments (all of this, done
to great effect). It's amazing how, with seemingly minimal
effort, Teal has conjured these fantastical and oft memorable
tales, all the while, never losing sight of the wondrous
scope and expansive power of temporal finitism. Truly, *We
Were Called Specimens* is on par with the warlock-suffused
brilliance of Alan Moore's *Promethea*, and even, the
undying and palpable mystique of Neil Gaiman's long-running

epic, *The Sandman.* I believe this is Teal at his finest."

—Mike Kleine, author of *Kanley Stubrick* and *Lonely Men Club*

"Jason Teal is an animal. Whether Marjorie is a platform, an alter ego, a would-be lover, or just product of his imagination, Teal finds a new way to define a character via these uncanny philosophies, experiments, and adventures. She is an indelible part of me now, having read her mantra. Thanks, Jason Teal, for this intrusion, this addition, this experience."

—Michael Czyzniejewski, author of *I Will Love You for the Rest of My Life: Breakup Stories*

"Yeah ... if I ever met a dick, it was Jason Teal."

—John Trefry, Inside the Castle

We Were Called Specimens
an oral archive of deity Marjorie

by Jason Teal

KERNPUNKT ● PRESS

Art: Cover: Matthew Revert
     Interior Art: Daniel Williams
Book Design: Jesi Buell

Excerpt from "A Tree or a Person or a Wall" from *A Tree or a Person or a Wall* by Matt Bell. Copyright © 2016 by Matt Bell. Reprinted by permission of Soho Press.

Excerpt from *The Red Goddess* by Peter Grey. Copyright © 2011. Reprinted by permission of Scarlet Imprint.

1st Printing: 2020

ISBN-13 978-1-7323251-7-3

KERNPUNKT Press
Hamilton, New York 13346

www.kernpunktpress.com

For someone else

"It is always easier to believe if you are opposed to something, or actually suffering for your beliefs. Without perceived or real oppression rebellion tends to sizzle—this is our current slack secular state in the West."

—Peter Grey, *The Red Goddess*

"When the boy could not stand to be alone in his head anymore—trapped inside this cracked skull trapped inside the locked room—then he sat up in the bed and turned toward the ape and made the only sound that still seemed sure.

EEEEECHHHHHSCRAAAAA, the boy said.

EEEEECHHHHHSCRAAAAA, the ape said back."

—Matt Bell, *A Tree or a Person or a Wall*

Table of Contents

Introduction

One blind spot (among many) in my literary study is that I have never developed a deep understanding of what we might call experimental fiction. Prose poetry. Heck, regular poetry, for that matter, if we're being honest about it.

Not that I don't comprehend its importance and have at least some awareness of both its utility and its necessity, but I'm not necessarily the best person to explain any of that to someone else.

I've learned from my experience with cinema that to really understand a form, you often have to acclimatize yourself to it. Not everything yields itself up to your first, clumsy ministrations. And with this sort of fiction, I simply haven't had enough experience to know the lay of the land just yet.

Which makes me an unlikely candidate to write this introduction, for the stories, vignettes, poems, what-have-you contained in this strange little puzzle box of a book are certainly experimental. Most of them are what I would call prose poetry. Sometimes broken out into discrete blocks of text—often replete with intentional repetitions that function like a Greek chorus, like call-and-response—other times one run-on paragraph that chokes much of a page, in each case, the form itself a part of the meaning of the piece in ways that I recognize, even if I can't explain.

But *We Were Called Specimens* is more than just experimental fiction—like any book, or story, or collection of stories, it is a great many things in one. Its subtitle calls it an "oral history," an account of the creation of a mythos; the birth of a universe. It is protest fiction, and resistance fiction, and literary fiction—and sometimes, as in "Simon Conjures the Dead" or "MurderLand" or "The Age of Death, An Account," genre fiction, as well. It is satire and subtext.

It is all of these things and more, and some of these things I understand better than I do experimental fiction, so perhaps that's why I'm here. To say, "Hey, even if you don't generally read stuff that's called 'prose poetry,' give this thing a shot. Don't be put off early on by the fact that the stories aren't what you're used to. Give the language a chance. It's often incantatory—it will lull you, if you let it, and it might take you someplace you've never been before."

That place may be a small cave or the edge of the universe, the Death Coaster™ or a burnt-through pasture "rocked by perpetual lightning storms we caused." Wherever it is, it will feel strangely familiar. It will tickle some half-awake part of your brain that tells you that maybe you have been here before, after all. In a dream, perhaps, or reading another book, some other time. Standing in line at the supermarket and waiting your turn, as your mind slipped into neutral while you stared at the headlines of the tabloids arrayed there to tempt you. Maybe you saw an article about Marjorie there…

\#

When I met Jason for the first time, it was because he had invited me down to Manhattan, Kansas to read from my latest collection. I say "down" out of habit, but actually it's more to the side and up, a drive out along I-70, around Topeka. If I were out east, I would have crossed a state or two. Here, I barely made a dent.

We had lunch at a pizza place and talked about writing and movies, about Kansas—where I had lived all my life and to which he was still a relatively fresh transplant—and horror practice. That's what I do, after all. I'm a horror writer.

We read scary stories at a coffee shop—myself and a handful of other writers—and drove through *Silent Hill*-like fog to continue our discussion at an IHOP at two in the morning, which seems like the thing to do in a college town.

Back then, I hadn't read anything that Jason had ever written, so we talked about the things that I had written, about movies and monsters and monster movies. The things I knew well.

In *We Were Called Specimens*, Jason writes about things that he apparently knows well—about the way our quotidian tasks become rituals, our rituals become mundane. The mythologies that we build to help ourselves cope with our march through life—and death—and the ways that we deny those mythologies.

Almost every story features the same handful of names—Marjorie, Leo, Simon, Rebecca—but they are jumbled around, plopped down in different places each time. Marjorie the goddess. Marjorie the exploitative aunt. Marjorie the pop culture phenomenon. Marjorie the Hand. Marjorie the failed salesperson. Marjorie the final girl. Marjorie the walking wounded.

In this way, each name becomes a kind of shorthand for all of us. We are all Marjorie, we are all Simon, we are all Leo, we are all Rebecca—or we know them, know someone like them. If not in this story, then the next one, or the next.

Themes bend and break from one story to the next as well, but they also recur and reform. Consumption. Denial. The distractions of modern living, and how they have ceased to be distractions and have become fundaments, necessities. "Everything hinges on the inner workings of the parade."

#

I said before that I knew the utility and necessity of experimental fiction, at least somewhat, and that's true, but here's something else I know: I know the importance of feeling seen. Of reading something and thinking, Yes, that's me, if only for a moment, if only for one line.

Earlier, I called the writing in *We Were Called Specimens* "incantatory," and it is, but an incantation needs a goal, doesn't it? This one is, ostensibly, an incantation to the deity Marjorie—but is it in praise of her, or an appeal for protection against her curse? Or is it both?

Whatever it is, it is also something else: a window or a mirror. Through its obfuscations and elisions, it lets us see clearly, and be seen, if only for a moment. That's something rare and special, even—and especially—when you don't understand it yourself.

Orrin Grey
December 2019

Orrin Grey is a skeleton who likes monsters, as well as a writer, editor, and amateur film scholar who was born on the night before Halloween. His stories have been published in dozens of anthologies, including Ellen Datlow's Best Horror of the Year, *and his writing on film has appeared in places like* Strange Horizons, Clarkesworld, *and* Unwinnable, *to name a few.* Guignol & Other Sardonic Tales *(Word Horde, 2018) is his third book of stories. John Langan once referred to him as "the monster guy," and he never lets anyone forget it.*

I Don't Feel Hungry in This World Anymore

Marjorie is born in the middle of a duster in Kansas.

Marjorie is born in Michigan in 1997, straddling three lakes.

Marjorie is born in Los Angeles in 1936, on a silver screen no one watches, sings haunted showtunes.

Marjorie is born in New Orleans in 1991, one day after her father is deployed to the Gulf.

Marjorie is birthed in Iowa; rumored sex magic.

Marjorie is born in transit, on a subway metro platform, but her mother vanishes without a trace.

Born in time for the end, pestilence, shaky buildings coming down in heaps.

Born in time for vacation, Marjorie catches the plane in the nick of time, her name called over the PA.

Born into mandatory retirement plans, second mortgages to fund college repayment.

Here on the island, before the reactor blows, Marjorie is born— then abandoned.

Marjorie is raised by wolves until the wolves die from super parasites.

Marjorie is raised high into the air, legs a-dangle over a hotel balcony, by her celebrity stepmother.

The small child suffers and sniffles alone in a burnt-through pasture.

No pretty pasture, mind you; this one rocked by perpetual lightning storms we caused.

We did not summon.

We did not speak.

We covet.

We scavenge.

We're crazy to explore the pasture, sure, but where else is there?

Imagine we needed answers, but the question is how to survive wave after wave of pandemic.

Marjorie'd better grow gills to live.

Marjorie'd better marry wealthy, and white.

As a rule.

You have to know where to take cover and when to run.

Marjorie is born in the pasture marked by oil derricks, where we hunt, hungry as wolves.

What luck for us today—she is lying where she is—plus this storm on our tails makes us hurry.

We have the baby Marjorie, but now what.

Our lips tremble.

Our ears wiggle.

Our throats swallow.

The right place at the right time, understand our luck; think about which animals passed her up for scarcer plates.

Our speech rambles.

Our thoughts wander.

Bigger animals than us, and with sharper tools, if they're smart.

Mangy fur and gnashing teeth.

Then we found her—no, we found her.

Quiet like a baby, so messed up.

In the tangle of trash below the hill, not our fault she's so messed-up looking.

Not our fault she's living in trash like that.

Not our trash; not that we can tell.

Maybe—maybe she's a little scrawny, or starved like us, and we even picked at dead things here and there.

Wonder how long she's not eaten, mossy stuff growing on her face.

Listen for volunteer breaths, words.

Nothing.

First we mistook her for a snake, faced in scales, lying in the trash like that.

Tiptoed around her, a little hiss.

The wind in approval.

Lightning on the wind, and our vision blurs.

Refocus, ready for the storm.

Marjorie stirs in our hands like she is asleep.

Marjorie stirs, probably smells lightning.

You develop a sense for lightning, like comfortable sounds at home.

Marjorie feels lightning approach, static discharge in our hands.

We almost drop her if the fungus didn't root across our hands, keeping her attached.

The fungus adapts to her stirring.

Wonder if that fungus improves her chances, camouflaged out here, but think she's dying soon.

With fungus cheeks, faces like the others.

Of course, there's always the guilt to deal with.

Comes with the territory—scorched—but a meal's a meal, and afterwards one of you is still living.

If not us, her.

If not her, another.

This child wouldn't be the first; trust us about the craving.

You take what you can get but the craving steals the show.

You feel the craving and now you act on the craving.

But you feel—you might feel like dirt for days afterward.

A gift laid in waste, her waiting there in the trash near the broken couch.

Laid in dirt, waiting for us like a gift, so she could taste like dirt.

No.

I mean I remember Marjorie tasted like dirt.

Look around for someone laughing, threat or enemy.

No one in this pasture lurking like us.

No one in this pasture holding free meat.

No one in this pasture urging squirming meat to silence.

No one in this pasture spying Marjorie in the dirt.

Awkward chortle.

What luck.

We have the baby Marjorie, but what is left.

I laugh sometimes at my own jokes.

I laugh sometimes at my own jokes when no else does.

I don't want to laugh at my own jokes.

I don't want to laugh at my own jokes but sometimes it happens.

We made up stories about Marjorie to wash her down.

Wash her down with poisoned water from the poisoned well—we're not picky.

We were so hungry—no one in sight and nothing left standing.

Everything dies eventually.

We kept weapons from home in case others grow wise, in case we give up.

For so long, the hunger panged our weak stomachs like xylophone teeth.

Trapped initially in the band room, we ate the xylophones.

Like for a long time we thought of candy, remember?

How the baby might have tasted of natural sugars.

No proof, but these candy lips and candy limbs were distracting.

Tear at the hair that hasn't fallen out; like plucking feathers from a chicken.

I mean we were consumed by thoughts of eating the sweet child.

Maybe she'd be crunchy, we thought, dirt hiding her from plain view.

Watched her ribs crack open with a sharp rock, then we ate like robbers; radioactive lungs warm like chestnuts, meaty bits spilled out in confetti rivers.

Faces rubbed green in nylon, from our crying, our sickly gums slapping.

Marjorie wrapped inside the puffer coat, all lit up and reborn as fuel.

We feel sick.

But we were reborn.

Her face glowed like a candlewick, stardust sunk in mud.

First Marjorie was born, then she really tried to live.

Marjorie lived for six hundred years inside of a small cave writing obscure language poetry and erotic novels.

Marjorie lived freely as an obstetrician's assistant in Toronto until the North American War of 2037, which was before the Second All-Continents War, which was before the Unsettled Corporate Farming Dispute of 2059.

Marjorie frolicked passionately with friends in 1961 in the apocalyptic commune, but they were besieged by the government for suspected occult activity.

It took a long time to eat her.

Our lips whistle.

Our ears got infected.

Our dead throats swell.

Our eyes seep pus.

Marjorie'd better cover up.

Marjorie'd better walk home with a friend at night.

Marjorie'd better respect police.

Remember bones snapping inside our mouths like fireworks.

We chewed on her tender meat in silence.

The power from the little savior excited us, so we shifted our privates like guns.

Because, we said, we survived this much, we ate the baby Marjorie.

Because, we said, we survived this much, we slept terribly.

The next day, we make the decision everyone is putting off.

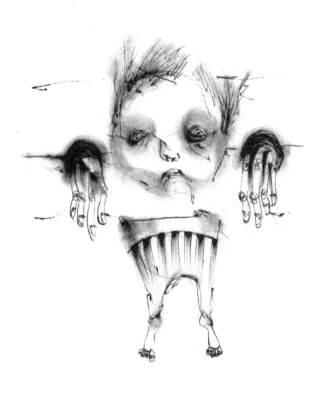

The Age of Death,
An Account

MY FIRST MONTH BACK FROM the dead and Aunt Marjorie starts touring cities, puts me on a ball and chain next to her podium for shows—THE AMAZING DEAD BOY REVEALS SECRETS OF HEAVEN!!! She prints these flyers and books food courts until we get national press, which happens after Leo calls in a favor from his friend in Los Angeles. Leo is promoted. His friend plus two staffers are hired full-time to manage my newly dead, hungry for brains persona.

The camp psychiatrist thinks I'm kidding about exploitation and when I tell her fame has fried Marjorie's brains, she ups my tranquilizers. Doping me keeps me from moaning about it. I pose for Suicide Girls, appear in pop videos. Meanwhile I stop eating with the crew, hide in my trailer.

I get a tutor who teaches me algebra—I'm hosting Jeff Foxworthy's Are You Smarter Than a Dead Person? pilot—and my famous aunt, in an interview with Oprah, consents to a televised check-up proving once and for all I have no heartbeat, that my skin is extra clammy. I eat my tutor.

Marjorie won't visit before tapings, gives Leo the keys to my restraints; I try to kill Leo five or six times, clawing at his face, but he finally screams the keys are fake when no one jumps in.

The thing is, I don't get paid for my jokes. I sit in writer's meetings, suggest scripts that broadly appeal to key demographics, where Leo pulls down salary plus benefits for wearing decoys. I almost gore him again out of spite. My not gutting him illustrates how death puts things in perspective.

Leo gets a book deal, leaves camp. The book never hits market and nobody hears from him again.

My aunt and her cronies scheme to hold me captive, ride out my miracle for all it's worth. I start to lock my trailer door; they unbolt it from the frame. I make it as far as the high school; they move me into stocks. I feel the restraints are reactionary, wasteful, but no one suggests how to boost the efficiency of their own torture.

The first thing to know about stocks is the drawn out feeling of time. But you knew that already. The second thing is the crew will stop to take photos beside your spectacle. Then the photos become Internet memes. Don't cry because it's over. Smile because you're not a walking stiff. Cowboys, no spittin' on scourge. Use spittoons. Cronies taunt me with them, direct orders from Marjorie.

Child Protective Services is tipped off anonymously but, on arrival, declares me legally dead. My aunt suspects Leo but says nothing more about it.

I am dead but not numb. Parts of me return to dust. News outlets publish leaked cease and desist letters from the state. They do not know what to do with me. Pundits ask viewers, Is this a failure of our representatives to act? Two interchangeable experts, pioneers in their respective fields, feud boyishly across different networks.

Some nights, I wonder about that word, scourge. It is the cronies' favorite slur to use on me. I don't fear it, though. I wear it like a festive sweater, laugh as their hokey insults come to depend more and more on the word.

I heard very little about my family word-for-word in camp. Only what my aunt told me. In the stockades, I filled in the gaps with what I could beat out of Leo. When my aunt found me she was living alone at my family's house. My dad had stopped responding and she was cleaning out the estate, putting his affairs in order as his power of attorney.

My dad drunk-drove me and mom into a ditch. He sleeps off his guilt, comatose.

I know my aunt favored Leo but his betrayal did not shake her opinion of him. Watching her run around camp, I wonder what she thinks about him. I'm afraid of what she'll say when I ask. We owe everything to Leo. Leo is our saving grace. Without Leo, where would we be?

My aunt says I showed up, out of nowhere, risen plain and simple, pounding on the door. I can't remember anything before she made me the soup.

Marjorie charges admissions for tours of the camp. Buzzards visit the camp like a dark bruise. We have a strong opening week, but no social media presence. We cannot survive on word of mouth alone. I tell my aunt this, "We cannot survive on word of mouth alone" and she says "That's a good point." She pays for an ad in the classifieds online. The copy describes Leo down to his pretty eyelashes. No one applies.

Advocacy groups for death rights picket the entrance and leak dramatic photos of me in the stockades. My aunt hires a security firm to keep them out.

Are You Smarter Than a Dead Person? is canceled after one season.

Leo's L.A. friend—his name, evidently, is Marcus—hears a more substantial offer from an advertising firm in New York, which he accepts without another thought. His staffers ditch us when he offers them competitive salaries with the firm. More and more volunteers abandon the camp. All of a sudden, my aunt is in charge of a sinking ship. She burns through her savings to feed the security firm that keeps the advocates at bay.

No one in television, radio, or other media wants to touch us, calls us a gimmickry of death. Death is so passé. It has been done and done and done and done. What else is there? What's our angle? My aunt is not a visionary. The miracle has run its course.

Plus, my perpetually rotting face is hard to maintain on top of this. The makeup artists fled last night, and my aunt's bad work has repulsed focus groups on more than occasion, if not because of the smell, a kind of burning plastic, then because it looks really gross.

I want to reason with my aunt. Leo is out of the picture. Why am I kept prisoner? I need out of the stocks. Someone sets up AV so we can watch the ball drop, runs extension cords plugged into a trailer so it reaches me. We are staying up for the New Year, and the mood is set, everything is primed for it, she even laughs at my dead boy jokes—I will suggest a few hours each day without restraints, you know, for good behavior—but then my aunt's friend Earl calls, screaming.

Earl says Stanley, the tutor, has risen in the city—biting strangers in the act. It's breaking news, have we turned on the set? We hadn't; Earl called before we sat down. Aunt Marjorie winces, holds the receiver away from her ear, feeling trapped or tired. I hear Earl's infrequent screams jump out of the phone.

—he screams here because a crow smashes into the patio sliding door, drops dead: Earl says the victims declined medical treatment, being uninsured or worse, unemployed, and now there is an epidemic extending to the valley, where we made camp—we are disconnected for at least another day.

Earl calls back, surprised he has service, a person's silhouette is standing on the lawn, looks lost, so Earl screams. Unable to tell whether or not someone is rabid—he calls them this, rabid—Earl has locked his door, turned out the lights. He says she is okay. He has ordered a new home security system with same-day installation. There was a special. Then the doorbell—Earl screams but it is probably just the technician. He hangs up.

I wonder why he chooses rabid to describe us. We are decidedly not living. There is something empowering about my kind rising up, taking vengeance. I'm not aroused, though, can't become erect, rotting. Instead: Earl stationed in front of his cameras, around the clock, sleeping there, sometimes trading posts with the technician, who saw some shit on the way over. I imagine Earl watching for any sign of death lurking in the brush, hilariously armed with a broom handle, a sharpened fire poker, and unafraid of strange dogs. Ricky, the technician whose name I have made up, has pepper spray—and a pistol in his glove box if things call for it, though he hasn't quite figured out how they'll flank someone to reach it in time. Neither plans to leave the house to find out. They aren't romantically linked, but circumstances are rife with a kind of productive tension.

This last time, Aunt Marjorie catches me eavesdropping. She looks at me sternly, mouths Are you listening to this, then pulls the phone back, and, walking away, mumbles a few consoling words into the phone, vague advice that pacifies no one, hangs up.

The next day Marjorie grills me about Stanely. Did I eat him? Of course I remember him. Don't I? S-T-A-N-E-L-Y. She spells it out, forwards and backwards, emphasis on each vowel. Her southern drawl flares when she is angry. I don't tell her she is spelling it incorrectly. I was frustrated, and Stanely provided an opening. I let out some steam. But I don't say that. I want out of the stocks. Instead I say, "Who is Stanely?"

The next day Aunt Marjorie says, "You remember the tutor, don't you?" I say nothing. She makes a face, another. She says, "When you ate the tutor, did you desire flesh? You wanted to wear around his thick tanned hide all hours like a coat." This one isn't even a question. "Did you wish to consume his essence, his soul? Tell

16

me." I say, "That's ridiculous."

Another day Marjorie tells me I'm lying. Her eyes seem to narrow on me, scrutinizing my dead, unmoving face. She says, "Did the Devil compel you to bite Stanely?" I say, "I didn't bite him." I'm lying. It doesn't matter. Marjorie moves into her RV, drives it across camp and parks it behind another useless structure.

Later, shouting starts outside the camp, where the poor advocates have stayed in tents or their cars. A guard sprints frantically past Marjorie's door. He is pursued by a rabid advocate. Scourge, as others would have it. Behind them, a pack has formed. They are loud, crass people not used to death. Marjorie's RV starts up, speeds off, deserts me in the center of camp, charges a few advocates slow to reanimate. This is the truth: My aunt flees camp, leaves me in the stocks.

I wonder what do you do to keep yourself occupied during the apocalypse. I don't have any answers. A buzzard descends, pecks at my face rot, but I can't feel it. I died when I was nine. I don't know anything, really.

After a couple hours, the buzzard has a voice, suddenly, baritone and imbued with song. He sings to me, songs of despair, murder ballads, country songs I can't listen to, not because I don't want the entertainment, a temporary friendship, just that the songs, I know for a fact, are poor imitations of something else. I haven't even heard "Busch Baby" in its original form and I know he is butchering it.

The buzzard has a greenish beak and its feathers are reddish, or the sun casts an eerie hue upon it. I ask it its name. The bird looks at me, sideways, perhaps annoyed that I cut him off mid-verse. It is snowing, or the buzzard punctures my cornea. His name, he says, is Simon.

Marjorie and the Mountain

MARJORIE STANDS AT THE BASE of a mountain, too afraid to climb. The mountain has the face of a man. It's her ex, an indifferent banker growing fat from poor people. No, it's her absent father. Her boss. Marjorie has bad luck dating men. Inside her bedroom, she sits on the suitcase until it clasps shut, collapsed from weight or time or both. Outside, she swings open her car door, shifts into drive, reeking of antibacterial formula, hands still smelling of work. Marjorie takes the points. She wants to leave, drive anywhere. She spins directly into the side of the mountain, totals the front end of her car. The doctor tells her living was extremely fortunate. She mumbles yes, yes, pays her copay.

Every day, Marjorie will work for ten hours for minimum wage. She carpools with Rebecca, an incompetent trainee. Each day the day ends, and that's it—she clocks out, feeds her sister's cat across town, never dusts, underwear in piles around the room. Waits for another day to pass. Waiting, falls asleep. Then she sleeps and sleeps. Almost sleeps through her morning shift if it weren't for Rebecca ringing her phone. Where is her phone? Marjorie hates her new immobile life. She can't pay the mechanic. He threatens junking the vehicle for scrap money. The mountain creeps closer until it is pressed up against her window, fogging the glass. Marjorie swears it breathes. The mountain erupted inside the neighboring complex at first, killing her neighbors instantly, but she was too depressed to notice. She thinks the mountain is expressive. Scott, her landlord, tells her there was an earthquake when it formed, but she didn't feel it—she slept through the event. He needs to inspect the property for damage or pets. Does she have rent. The next morning, the fire trucks blocked her in. Then and only then Marjorie sees the mountain for what it is, its hunched ridge looming spectacularly in her back yard. She doesn't have a back yard but means something by this expression. She can't remember what.

The mountain hoped to make an entrance, some grand gesture. Instead it barely sprouted like a runt daisy. Here, the mountain strikes her as an inconvenience, not a natural wonder. The mountain begins to grow into Marjorie's window, close enough so she can feel its heat. She wonders if it will bloom lava. The mountain pushes spider webs of cracks into the window glass, an unadorned Christmas reef. It is summer. Any day, tourists are stopped to take photos in front of the busted window, their voices carry in the shadow of the sudden landmark and keep Marjorie awake. People drink alongside the mountain and leave empty bottles all over the street. A festival is organized in honor of the mountain. The town votes on a name for the mountain no one uses. The mountain's too slight to encourage much climbing, but down the street, an old man raises a placard above a rusty cart, proclaiming Magic Mountain Souvenirs open for business. He sells shirts and keychains, anthropomorphic hats. Legends are forged. Marjorie hears them circulating outside on the street. The mountain has been raised by dead gods. Of course. Marjorie can't believe in magic, just coincidence. One night, fractured star light sprinkling into her room around her, she reaches out to touch the cheek of the mountain, but the mountain jumps aside, killing everyone it runs over, which isn't as sad as when as the first time. Life goes on.

Marjorie Saves the School

MARJORIE SAVES KIDS FROM SCHOOL shootings. Disciples of Leo are infiltrating schools to make examples of children and Marjorie ducks into the science lab to take the armor-piercing rounds instead. When she is done absorbing bullets, we lay her down in the hospital bed and our teachers execute the mentally-ill disciples. The life-saving surgery is live-streamed across social media and aired on major networks, but Marjorie can't watch the fruits of her labor. We don't know if she'll pull through. In class, surviving children re-enact the martyr's swooping action, wrapped in gauze and hooked up to life support. Her image is smelted onto our guns and national currency, but Leo continues to incite hate crimes, holed up in a cave in the desert. Our school shootings increase so we arm the children, outfit kindergartners for flak jackets. We never asked Marjorie if she were bulletproof.

The Condition of Marjorie's Feet

MARJORIE IS TELEVISED. SHE IS a divining rod for all miracles, the plants and the animals and the crude oil. See Leo stand again, once paralyzed from drunk driving. He hasn't walked in fourteen years. It's all there on video, sermons from $9.99 plus $5.99 shipping and handling. One hundred years from now, the Lord will tarry, and we will sing "In Christ Alone" in the same church at Christmastime, resolves tested by plagues of war, disaster, famine, and death. Marjorie has foretold the exact date of his second coming, and we request off work.

Marjorie's nephew Simon is possessed after school: The exorcism is filmed same day before a live studio audience, and Marjorie only speaks in tongues. Subtitles are unavailable. Later, she begs his mother to pull him out of school. We believe in the power of ritual, and we believe in Marjorie. See her tongue loll out like a plump snake: right there, the demon invades her spirit. Her nephew is fine and Marjorie convulses on stage like an epileptic. You aren't looking. I hope you too can be saved.

Marjorie is a divining rod for weather, routing storms to islands full of heathens. Those people do not know grace. But they will learn. Apply for missionary work. Send us your money, and Marjorie will pray, and God will break up marriages between friends and coworkers. His grace alone comes through faith alone in Marjorie alone. We love homophobes. We love gay people. We love black people. We are homophiles. We will take anyone transformed by the message of the spirit. Our church welcomes all people, regardless of race, creed, or gender. Bring a credit card and a valid photo ID or proof of residence. Our members are exceptional. Our facilities are tremendous. We await salvation here, digging in for the long haul, we each have our own bunker for the apocalypse.

We are stewards of Marjorie. Stalwarts of tradition. Marjorie has the penthouse suite, and she will deliver us unto Heaven. We are unworthy of such grace. We grovel at Marjorie's unwashed feet, kissing the corns. She walks everywhere, and we are not surprised. Marjorie says we don't need money to be happy. She has the governor's ear, palmed and wriggling on stage. Marjorie is magic, and we don't question results. Marjorie will restore the country to glory, glory. She names progressives who reject core doctrines and we burn down their churches.

Marjorie has three marriages in three years because her partners failed to see the all-knowing light. It wasn't murder. All debts are forgiven on death. All life matters, Marjorie roars on, using member testimony, and during sermon, we agree life begins at conception. We burn down the clinics. We don't use contraception, we move to South America. We don't tell our families and we won't be prosecuted. Send us your money, and Marjorie will pray, and God will buy Marjorie a private jet. She charters flights for senators to expensive resorts. We will hide in the mountains, asking God to forgive Leo, and of course he will beat cancer.

Our church stateside has less than three hundred members. We don't listen to praise metal, we don't use light shows or smoke machines, and Marjorie isn't a celebrity in the tabloids. We don't read the tabloids. Instead, we marry, we bury lovers, we baptize sinners—we hope to love our politicians as we love ourselves. Listen: What you see on television is not who we are.

Marjorie Will Ride the Death Coaster™

MARJORIE WILL RIDE THE DEATH Coaster™. Marjorie will ride the Death Coaster™ to prove her gusto. Marjorie was diagnosed with brain cancer. She would like to prove her gusto, she says, to banish the malignant tumor. The Death Coaster™, a strata coaster, changed lives from almost 500 ft in the air, baptisms surpassing the height of other rides. When we arrive, the Death Coaster™ is closed. The Death Coaster™ is down for scheduled maintenance.

Returned, we will say our friend Marjorie challenged brain cancer and amusement park lines for the Most Dangerous Ride™ on the same day. We make a pact on the car ride home, listening to Marjorie's annoying mixtape. No one sings along.

At the funeral, we repeat this story for family and friends.

Expiration

TIME HAS TO LET MARJORIE go. They are very sorry, they tell her, but she's trapped inside the minute—and possibly, very soon, she could fall prey to the second. She is infinite in the dogless dog park.

History repeats itself, Marjorie counters, but Time, uncaring, has vanished already. Dogs expire all around her, in sister cities, slumped dead onto lawns, one of them smiling. Later, their humans mourn privately in bed, fantasizing about lost puppies or lovers. Time, of one mind, lays waste indiscriminately.

Marjorie looks around at nothing, green rolling back, back, back into memory; she floats above the turbulent flow, watching dust storms level her hometown and flood surrounding counties.

Time is bureaucratic, formless. Marjorie is human and different.

She stays looping nameless green until another interstellar body, the planet Simon, pulls her closer with a bigger gravity. He can't talk, mute from Time. Lightyears on lightyears and almost out of fuel, Marjorie and Simon see the universe scooped inside a black hole. This shrinking world happens one summer expedition.

Simon chews on the cross necklace and Marjorie watches, rapt. She loves him in bible school, memories idling nearby, Simon suckling on the dangled cross like a constellation.

Hurt inside and out, she is weaker now more than ever, ripe for capture. The microworld assails her, latches on to her yellow dress, the earth in her breath. Simon holds Marjorie, laughing while they tumble out of orbit, the red shift of summer burning dogbones to a crisp.

He shoves Marjorie, once, hard. Alone, Marjorie heats the infinite void with wilted hands, crouched over and blaming science. Without Simon, there is no one—

Another thing about Time: it's a very intimidating pace. This is why it should only be visited once.

Watching stars etch meaning into blackened dust, she slips further into forgetting—a blanket whiteness spreading over the park.

Subdivision

THE FRIENDLY SKY FROWNS AT Marjorie; the blue sun sets dramatically on nowhere, bathing nothing in darkness. There is no moon. An eclipse of the country. A century passes. Another.

The next day, developers, fat with money and lacking creativity, see the nothing Marjorie occupies—"LIVE: homeless epidemic on TV!" "Breaking interviews with residents of 1400 Crescent faced with population surge." Another boring documentary with a message; the box office suffers, scares studio execs. The execs hire the developers to renovate their new Vermont homes. A project to distract, a project to raise property values until the scum leave Crescent St.

The renovation takes a century. And another.

Credits roll after the centuries; the developers sleep periodically (without pay) and dream of the dark dark. This dark worms into basements, abandoned cars, the open mouths of teenagers. That night, the developers dream Marjorie standing inside of the dark. Inside Marjorie is confused, hungry, and stumbling through oblivion. Shaky breaths. Camera jiggles once, twice. Fade to black. Cut suddenly to Marjorie's shoes, carnival music, discarded prizes. She stands alone. Simon, Leo, others approach; everyone wanting for something, arms locked against time.

The developers, working over, build a house inside the house, orders handed down. The execs have moved on, leaving the house site abandoned indefinitely. They are missing with no leads. The police scratch their heads. But the house stays. The house breeds houses. No one lives nowhere. Marjorie and the residents stand house-adjacent, lost in argument. They can't make up their minds: Demo by explosives? Who rents out construction equipment at this hour?

The house eats Marjorie and Simon and Leo and everyone in the neighborhood. The house organizes the other houses. The house grows bigger and bigger, eats people's mailboxes, traffic, the other houses, youth centers. The house, imposing like a fortress, eats the school and the kids inside. It eats the homeschooled.

Another century. The richest flee underground. The house moves on to another block.

The richest send lawyers, fearing death, disorder. Cease and desist. The house eats the lawyers. The richest, wild underground, flee into the woods, smelling air for the first time in centuries. The house eats the woods and the small businesses, it eats the banks and the hotels. The house eats the box stores with the clearance items, the plants and all the animals, but only the developers weep.

Dumped by Marjorie

I OFFERED MARJORIE PEARLS. She didn't want pearls. I bought a lobster caviar frittata in New York, gold leaf-wrapped sushi in Manila. She picked around her food. She asked me to drive her to Portland. Then she lost her train ticket. I chartered a flight. She didn't like waking up early to check in. She slept through her alarm. I told the pilot to keep the plane taxied. I called Marjorie a cab. The union was on strike. She didn't trust my drivers or my classic cars. I put her in an Uber. She said she missed economy seating, meeting people. I paid friends to fly across the country. She didn't board, nervous about airport security. I tried, curtly, to describe my real estate holding company in Seattle. I would set her up in a trendy condo. She snorted, wheezing on the phone. She didn't like my wealth, she said. She described me as a very dead corpse, prone to decay. I was on my deathbed and Marjorie and I fell into this fight. One of us kept leaving, blaming, hating, cursing the other. I didn't hear from her for two years. I was still living. She changed shifts, her nephew needed someone at home. I hired a private eye to investigate. His tail turned up nothing of importance. She found out I hired the detective. She said, The rich are at a special disadvantage. Because of the nature of wealth, she said, you will die sooner. Marjorie said, You are spoiled into weakness, your lungs sticky with bile. I said, That cancer's from smoking, not greed. She said, I hope you die wicked slow. After, she started wearing the pearls. She moved to Boston. She goes by Jorie now. She said, No one can hear you cry out, my rasping scratching yips delivered into the skin of her pillow.

Exceptional Air

MAYBE THIS NEW YORK IS a scale model of that New York, cut from steel sheets to 3D museum quality when fully assembled, no glue or solder needed, so Marjorie buys the $49.99 starter kit from a craft store she never frequents, an unremarkable store except for her nephew worked summers here during college, and now he lives in real New York, and although she has never visited, Marjorie has seen enough movies to know she won't.

Of course, Simon never bothered to fly her out, either.

Maybe Marjorie lives a solitary life bookended by Family Feud reruns, spending painstaking hours in front of the set trying to put the city together, but small parts keep breaking off or falling under the couch through her indelicate hands, and while the model keeps getting bigger and more expensive each return trip to the craft store, each addition costing more than half as much as the starter kit, Marjorie sometimes has to ask the nice kid, whose ears remind her of Simon, which of the expansion kits she doesn't have.

Soon she has to move her favorite chair from the living room into the dining room, pushing the dinner table up against the wall just for somewhere to sit. She has arthritis. The leaf makes this hard going.

Maybe the box says ages fourteen and up, but Marjorie feels small and insignificant, head shrunken because of onset dementia, spending days and nights lost inside the city, building boroughs and power lines, encircled inside of heaps of small parts labeled carefully by number and letter—she considers buying a dresser online to sort these, but reconsiders because she has no actual space to keep another dresser, so she removes her clothes from her clothes dresser and sleeps on her clothes, which are on top of her bed. She loses her socks. Instead wears slippers soggy from overuse.

Glue is in her hair but she hasn't used glue, it must be something else. She doesn't take time to smell it, hasn't showered in weeks, and she can't smell anything herself, olfactory senses numbed to the conditions of living within the fake city.

Marjorie opens the bag of food for the cat, so if the cat wants food, then it can eat food, because she can never seem to find the bowl in this mess of urban sprawl. She loses the cat. One day, Marjorie sees the bulk of the food pile hasn't shifted in weeks, looking intently at it from behind the model airport, all flights delayed because of snow. She scours New York, trudging through snow and traffic to find her cat, a goner for sure on these mean streets, but a lifelong friend all same, as many years as the cat breathed anyway. She puts him at one hundred twenty-five in cat years. Marjorie figures she owes him this much—if not a clean litterbox, then at least a safe home.

Maybe no one in the city will talk to Marjorie and so she can't find her cat, forgetting to eat for herself. She lives nights and days inside of the walls inside of the fake model city. She can't feel her legs, numbed from walking miles around calling her cat's name, hanging up flyers with photos of the cat, a phone number for the phone Marjorie isn't standing nearby and doesn't have an answering machine for. She hasn't been eating or taking prescriptions the doctors write instructions for, thinking these doctors mucked up the story of her body, but she is too far away for the pills upon pills to make any difference now. Above her in the rain, the waxy American soap opera shimmers, neon signs casting piss colors across slush running into street gutters.

Inedible Human Food

THE FARMER'S MARKET IS HARD going. Marjorie's chickens lay valuable eggs no one wants. Jade eggs, mother of pearl, porcelain trinkets mislabeled as heirlooms—perhaps, Leo says, it hinges on the cycle of the moon. He hasn't slept for weeks, determined to win his video game.

But he's wrong. There's no telling because of the weather. Suitable buyers exist. When the eclipse dips low over prairie wilds, hiding funnel clouds stalking nearby hamlets, the chickens drop Styrofoam peanuts. Rain: black licorice. Another rain: the skulls of baby snakes.

What goes in never comes out. There's no rhyme or reason, but Marjorie, thinking always of her nephew Simon—and sometimes of Leo warfighting at home—cares for these chickens. She returns to the market Saturday after next with her wares, sale or no sale, weekend after weekend after weekend. But she will never eat the thin chickens, excreting untold lives from unknown worlds. Each one has a name, a different personality.

At the farmer's market, she is the last to arrive but she is the first to leave everything behind her, thoroughly annoyed with shoppers.

It goes like this until Frankie the Silkie collapses mid-roost. In the morning, his frayed feathers have been ceremoniously plucked off. Not long after, Henrietta the Australorp croaks mid-crow. She had been more vocal recently, leaving the coop over and over without reason as if testing predators to strike out from behind cover. It was never clear where in the fence Henrietta escaped, the border undamaged, the dirt unraked. Mute Rebecca across the way, miles over, walked her back like a child's lost toy every afternoon—limply but noticeably tender.

Then the stink of death when the rest of the flock runs squawking flat into the side of an unfinished parking structure. They fall off the edge of the pit, dug for support beams, and into a mess of metal and wires. The viral video captures them howling furiously like menaced senators, probably chased but it is too hard to tell. The position of the poster causes glares from the sun. Leo recruits Simon for war: He laughs and laughs every time Simon says something hilarious on the game about chicken brains. The shrill joy of dumb boys cuts so deep into Marjorie she has to lie down. She can hear simple anatomies falling through precious construction like murder for hours.

Lately even Simon rolls his eyes and pinches his nose when she comes near, taking cues from Leo. In the bedroom, she hurts alone for these chickens. Lightweight water clings to her cheeks like weather.

All night there is the dream: The sun lights her path, then dims. She calls out once to Simon, eating her words, overcome with concern for falling rocks. The sun is setting, rolling backwards across the gorge. Marjorie crawls forward, help screamed nowhere overhead, Simon shouting for no one or lost. Simon tearing through the forest with or without Marjorie's pack. Had she fallen alone, dragging herself along rainwater in sputtered starts, nails thick with mud? That much is unclear. The water is inches deep at the bottom of the dusky ravine, and cold. She remembers two bodies or more tumbling down. Suddenly Leo is pinned inside jagged rocks to her right, breathing hard. All considered, the longer Marjorie looks the more the damp version of Leo resembles nothing alive.

She doesn't wake with a sweat. Instead she takes the first thing she can reach for out of the room. She remains at the farmer's market until after close. The boys must be hungry.

Almost Human

WE WERE CALLED SPECIMENS. WE learned human sign language in captivity, hid meanings in code. We built tools for torture.

Marjorie left our brother, stone dead, in the desert. Brutal sun cooked her RV like prime rib. We said adrenaline carried Marjorie from state to state: Slinking out of the cab, Marjorie felt abandoned by animal bodies.

We were ghosts, scratching our bottoms. We said cash only, "One night. Smoking or nonsmoking?"

We said in exit interviews, "We were never unhappy at our jobs." Chimpanzees laughed at our own jokes.

We said in historic times, "Mating rituals last ten to fifteen seconds."

The AC bleated its miserable song. What happened to animals in close quarters. In the room. We were called specimens.

We said in orbit, "We can't grasp changes in altitude without snacks or reward." Chimpanzees died in orbit.

There were instructions with our brother: Give him constant care. Almost human. His animal body wrapped inside a blue tarp and buried in the desert. His frame did not eclipse four feet, but he fought all the way to the ground.

Chimpanzees weren't strange because we knew sign language, not at first. We smiled at Marjorie, bared teeth. We said we saw this erased in a second.

We said we saw this erased in a second, "Marjorie erased this shining beaming thing, and we knew grief."

We were hunted for bush meat. In our habitat loss. Chimpanzees get eaten. We were called specimens.

We said in hard times, "We're gonna be sick." Bugs in the RV. We ate the bugs. We were dead.

We live sixty years. In captivity. In the wild, forty. There were receding spaces. We lived there. Our animal bodies.

The animal body confused Marjorie. Petite. In the room. The A/C resets, rattles.

We said Marjorie couldn't sleep. Through the night. Wrapped in blankets like a tarp. We levitated her.

We said Marjorie struggled. We said in the darkness, "We hoot, grunt, and scream."

We said in sports, "We have opposable thumbs. We go first." We were gone.

The Other Side of
the Mirror of Lies

MARJORIE SPIT SEEDY NIGHTMARES FROM the face of the black mirror. I crept nervously around the house, hating floorboards, countertops. I banged my knee and cursed. If I lied, she probably heard it. Then some rain. I watched the garden sprout trophy crops. I kicked myself red with envy. Said I forgot miracles worked better than routine labor. I said the dog died of cancer. In the meantime, the summer house foreclosed. I quit my job at the fracking firm as soon as brunch.

"I won't tell you everything," I said, biting my nails, reduced to chipped edges, but I was talking to a ghost. Her time was precious. She was missing for months then declared dead. At the wake, we mourned appropriately.

The mirror was a gift. Arrived unpolished with no sender, so I scoured the empty face, twice, checking for ruptures. In the heated garage, clear-seeing and supranormal, I slit the film wrap with rusty scissors, waxed the cold black of my doom with a work rag. Something inside me balked at Marjorie's divine visit, pimply and exposed. I wasn't high or drinking, but the appearance of my lover gave me pause. We observed silence.

Later, I blotted my eyes with the candied patchwork of an injured towel. I leaked sadness. Madness, more likely. Colleagues were up and had gone to church, but for me it was so early and bright.

I didn't have the fear of god but, when Marjorie was hard up, she almost loved me. I didn't believe her, not for her trying. Unexpected travel from the afterlife made a bold statement to the living. Another, darker thought: She owed me nothing. I had been cursed for my part in her death. All of it.

Marjorie moved designer armchairs onto the ceiling. She flung harmful chemicals against the walls, fanning noxious fumes around my apartment. She found my LPs and unceremoniously sunk them in brownish bathtub water. In minutes, my LPs and the bath water vanished.

My hands searched her face for answers, secret lives. An old letter from Marjorie read I was better off alone. My eyes pierced its cryptic ink splatter. I kept a rigid code. I was not allowed or even supposed to mention that letter. I burned the letter. Best I didn't think of her at all.

Marjorie had no sister; I was a convert. An itchy mystery. I occupied a spooky noir while I rowed with the disembodied voices overhead. I remembered the knife in the upstairs bathroom, considered death. But I craved life in all its enormity. I shouted promises I couldn't keep, if only she would leave me alone. The fact was, Marjorie never called. She never said someone I used to love tried to throw me off the bridge. There was no paper trail—no prepared testimony, anyway.

There was Marjorie talking and then a snort. A loogie, and I caught everything. It was more than one—she was coughing streams of it into a napkin in the other world.

My steps upstairs were heavy, clownish. I let the mirror collect dust until it didn't.

Simon Conjures the Dead

BABY . . . MARJORIE HATES ME. HONEY, sweetheart, my sugar . . . Retching starts. Darling . . . Other voices, mocking. I'm glad we ran into each other. Never met before. I was saying. Look into Madame's psychic eyes. Marjorie, listen to me. Medium can't breathe from the occupation. Meet my gaze. Dead calm. That time before. Real low, the medium cracking. I loved. Not the same you. It's complicated. Marjorie's almost out of reach. Marjorie is here with us. Don't move. Stop, say it. Same time tomorrow. Clockwork, unwound. I have this belief. Don't try that. The planchette moved. No one talks. Absence of heaven. I saw everything. I healed you. Possession, brief. There's a lot of time until we can move. I froze. Marjorie is here with us. Madame this time. There's a whole school of trouble, if you wait. I should go. The doors. Slammed. Locked. Doors bolted, Madame mounts the table. I will boil your face skin, peel it from your skull. Escalation, near death. The blood will spray from your earholes. Unrealistic. A fourth meal. Someone's hungry for—broken plate zips into the floor. I don't understand. Madame worms along the floor. A hundred fiery. She can't finish. I'm leaving. The floor overrun by hell beetles. Goodbye love. I don't love you. Love awake for centuries. Marjorie is here with us. Take my bicuspids, worn from chewing. I won't. Take my tongue, sick of licking roomy bosoms. Madame has scissors, holds out her tongue, plump and red. Wrestled gone in the stores of mankind. She was only performing—a taunt. "Scissors." She holds up scissors, cuts away.

Marjorie's in the Basement

MARJORIE DID NOT STAY IN the basement. We put her there for our safety. Turned off the lights. Forgot dinners. Because of the accidents. There were accidents with birdwatchers, neighbor toddlers falling into koi ponds, missing family keepsakes, deleted voice-mails, the Kincaid painting zooming once into a lit fire, bent utensils Leo used to rescue the Kincaid from the fire, slamming office doors, too-snug blankets holding us down, inconvenient weather; then the missing toddler investigations by police, sudden-ugly sisters, dead pets turning up on doorsteps, awful holiday dinners with in-laws, poetry open mics, Sunday brunches, dumb comedy movie nights Leo organized (none of us laughed), becoming lost on hikes, hiking, bad barbecue, parking (Marjorie blocked us in), missed appointments (her car blocked us in), late utility bills, our wardrobe smeared with feces. All the blood in empty rooms. So we blamed Marjorie. Journalists camped on the front yard. This attention was an accident. We didn't want her at first. Marjorie was a burden. We cannot stand accidents. This is why we put her in the basement. We believed she would stay put. We lived in the country. We hoped everyone grew bored.

Skin Fall Dandy Collection for Him

SIMON WEARS THE TRENDY LINE particularly dark. His lurid stare evoked shock and despair in rehearsals. He could have any job he wants, rumor has it, but this is the job everyone wants. His legs feel the way water drips, drips. As he falls, he remembers a recent death in the trades, his hair guy Leo, a former runway idol hired for notoriety, not because he was very skillful or liked much by anyone in the industry—but the surge in publicity afterwards was an easy opportunity at the time. Now smartphones keep Simon's epicene spill in focus, authenticating each heavenly twitch of the disassembled model, thinking viral, viral, not the routine he and the designer envisioned over encrypted video chats. Not the routine Simon played over and over in his head before curtain call. It is his time to flaunt, but with each half-step Simon flails uncontrollably atop the platform. Arms and legs in free spasm, a seizure, as if he were falling from an airplane—so unlike his trademark grace—the skin suit overrides his motor skills and splits him. The once-quiet audience licks their gore-slicked faces before roaring together, climbing over bleachers, ropes, and each other in the frenzied splatter, grabbing for their favorite parts.

Even Simon had to spend ten or so minutes squeezing into the tight, leathery piece backstage. The hides of different animals stitched together, he thought, exotic wares from an unidentified country. Nobody quite knew. But it was hot. Simon never suspected a spell would sever him. A nano-explosive. Somebody put a mechanism in the suit no one would trace in the autopsy. Maybe he ingested the device. A whistleblower, the designer stayed mum on his resources for the fall line. Most assumed an inheritance cultivated his eccentricities. He only selected the fairest-white models for his campaigns, against public outcry, and you didn't complain when you were chosen. Meeting the designer had not set off alarm bells between Simon's ears. Now everything was ringing, smoky. When pressed, the designer described his supply as "recyclable" and "vintage." Of course Simon never apologized.

Someone flexes the model Simon's fabulous thigh muscle off stage and eyes up the catwalk, determined to conquer his abandoned routine. It wasn't Simon's choice, his body spread in tatters at the mercy of the crowd. One of Simon's loose eyes spins so it briefly faces the other. A dashing paparazzi's haste to witness the carnage offers Simon this cross-eyed view: each new body part elicits a fawning scream from the elite crowd. Two adolescent girls club each other with his noodle arms. Simon's stringy meat feels plopped off one at a time, separated from his now-gelatinous skin as the fans steal fistfuls, soft shoulders floating off the stage into pools at the people's feet. He can't talk if he tried. He has no lips: he catches sight of a journalist wearing them on her forehead like a third eye, scribbling furious notes. He has trouble breathing, his left lung parachutes from his ailing body into the darkness, but the crowd hollers like they have just seen payday. Correctly preserved, intact limbs and intestinal rope could only appreciate in value on the black market.

Later, the stage manager Marjorie tosses his remaining parts—a cauliflowered ear, his nipple ring, other disturbing bits—off of the catwalk. She wishes leftover Simon good luck with everything. Airport chatter pulses blackly in and out of focus. The rest of Simon sits unpossessed alongside the catwalk, scattered to the crowd, walked through, as a skin hungry producer operates his signature flair in pieces for online viewers, fans with their own slaughter standing by for personal interviews. Simon feels the bridge of his nose rub against the boundary of the catwalk, then ricochet into his lonely eyes, kicked away by a cameraman who needs this angle for the rest of the show, a blurry shape huffing out of breath from the effort, watching as the next queued model stomps hatefully through the slimy tale of Simon and onto stardom.

Chores

THAT SUMMER WHEN WE FOUND the clearing, our school friend Marjorie remembered she had chores at home and escaped without harm, but the rest of us stayed and played awful pranks with sticks in the shallow bed, pushing each other against the mossy rocks or farther into the brackish runoff, tasting polluted favors of the town as several shadows bubbled up and out of the fast-moving river. We watched one black wave drag Leo under its foam mouth, a reluctant sacrifice for the monsters in the deep feeding on that hollow body, pumping our legs and arms frantically against the wake, the rest of its clan slashing at our exposed ankles with invisible knives as we scrambled ashore one by one, bleeding from our grateful scabbed knees, understanding full well why Marjorie had abandoned us in the clearing and what we had to do.

Everyone to Blame

IN THE PAST, WHEN BODIES turned up, or there were kidnappers, officers arrived on TV, badges glinting, to arrest the suspect. Marjorie is missing at the proctologist's office, her job as the office assistant. Maybe you are a suspect still.

Marjorie looked guilty. You remember that. You wish the phone receiver scalded her ear; you wish flames snaked across curled wallpaper like insects. You wish anything else happened, even if everything burned through and you had to start all over.

The call comes late at night, police knocking on your door. None of this seems real. No one has seen your boyfriend Simon for three days. Someone messed with his house, someone opened his mail, and last night, police found his truck, abandoned, with two slashed tires. Someone left dismembered doll parts in the truck bed. When you answer, you're wearing one shoe, desperate for news. You're lucky to wear one shoe considering you're alive. Lying in the grass that night, the pieces don't make sense: You lived with Marjorie and Simon's dead and now you're all covered in guilt. You survived.

This morning, the front door was open again. Put the chair back where it belongs. The kitchen smells like turpentine, scrubbed clean. So they found Simon, buried in the woods. You're wanted for questioning. What's the point of changing homes anymore?

It's not your fault, said Marjorie. Remember she kept disappearing. They picked her up in Colorado once, heading west in a stolen RV. Simon had already been missing for weeks. Now there is a mini-series named for her (which is better than the independent movie from a few years before). Online forums dissect her memory. Here is one more reason: Marjorie was evicted previously for bogus claims of racket, records played too loud, high-pitched moaning and screaming. No one could guess what the song was supposed to be. Other applicants didn't return your messages. In the interview Marjorie said, "I don't even listen to music, like ever." She was dressed typically in ripped blue jeans and a tie-dyed shirt, poor dreadlocks, wardrobe screaming Trustafarian.

Learn to trust yourself with time, purging Simon's emails, little tokens planning love sprees, poems, inexpensive dates. Anyway: Marjorie stuck the note to your fridge, letters pasted together from magazines. The series didn't capture her dark quiet. "I am dead tired," you said one night unremarkably, but Marjorie stared at you too long, unconvinced, so you offered, "We can watch something else." She made two cocktails, sweet mixes tasting like summer. You passed out hating work tomorrow, bingeing favorite cartoons and missing everyone from home. You didn't tell anyone Simon still lived in town. Later, police think Marjorie picked up the phone, her voice springy like a used mattress. Your phone was in the kitchen. Remember—Marjorie helped you burn his photos a few days afterward. She kept a collection of old dolls.

You never go into her room.

At the morgue, you are shown the lobby. In here is cold tiles, old magazines stuck to each other. The room smells bad, and you can't find a clock. It's nowhere.

Meat Debt

THERE WERE THREE COWS GRAZING in the field next to an airport. Marjorie stopped the RV, the engine idled beside the pasture, and a logging truck, followed by a mid-sized sedan, rolled past slowly, unsure if Marjorie was broken down or just grabbing pictures. None of the garish flank of bumper stickers—snarky messages advocating peace, where to put your cell phone, honor roll—applied to her anymore. She wore these labels dispassionately, shrugging off certain memories once Simon's kidnapper sent a toe, then a finger, then an ear.

The logging truck was late for its delivery, but the dad driving the mid-sized sedan decided not to pull over, suspecting hitchhikers for murders, parked RVs for drug-crazed hippies or inbred monsters cooking meth (he only started watching new TV a few weeks ago).

At the intersection, tailgating the logging truck, the dad hits the brakes when the truck brakes suddenly. The family veers off the road and into a ditch. How many stomachs does a cow have? One of them was lying down, shot in the field because it was sick. The other two were eating it.

Service

IN AMERICA'S MALL, INSIDE A kiosk erected with hungry yet selfish people in mind, endures Marjorie who can't sell anything. A line of camels goes schlepping by.

Marjorie works for an international multi-level marketing company selling nutritional supplements, weight management, and personal-care products, her script discarded atop fitness magazines she shoplifted from the bookstore. She wishes for the kiosk to burn down with everything in it, herself included. She is so bored.

She drops the script to consider the bomber planes zooming overhead, forgets about burning. The planes' sharp mouths seem to cut through exposed sky.

Her commission suffers, but still she asks, Free sample? and you say No please, switching shoulders for your purse, looking for the nearest bathroom, panicked but shopping unsuccessfully for discounted sweaters.

Marjorie knows where the bathrooms are, if you bothered to ask. She has closed the stand five times already, between trips to the food court, the arcade, and the bathrooms, working and not working to upsell bystanders. The camels move deliberately slow without riders.

Marjorie clasps and unclasps her shoplifted watch, unsure of her morning exit: She stole clean underwear from her girlfriend Rebecca because she hadn't done laundry. She will sneak them back someday, fully laundered. The bomber planes look rehearsed for an air show no one reviews online.

Marjorie hates the kiosk job: The people lately never stop and she has forgotten which supplements are for which precondition, the bottles this same blurring green stripe with matching font. The camels die expectedly from thirst. The mall fountain has been out of service for three weeks, rumors of a special part unavailable from the manufacturer.

The shifts were part time, so Marjorie sells Mary Kay door-to-door to supplement her income, but no one answers their doors for twenty-five dollars and under. She leaves print catalogs stapled to her card in the door cracks. Her sales plateaued last quarter, the number unchanged from her nephew charging an electric razor by accident.

There was trouble with steady income. The wrong credit card could crumble Marjorie's life, and often it did. She was always mentioned in letters from creditors, phone messages to wrong numbers. The bomber planes are shot down out of the sky by surface to air missiles, built by their own government. One of them burrows into the ground next to the brand-clothing outlet.

Marjorie considers diving under the counter of the kiosk, hearing artillery fire. She ducks, taking two slugs in her right calf. Bullets whiz by her ear and through the thatched roof of the kiosk. Bleeding, she lays back remembering that morning: Rebecca had made coffee, which was a kind gesture—she sees her smile through excruciating pain—but she forgot the mug on the roof of her car pumping gas, and Marjorie couldn't find the mug again going into work, the bold green polo marking her ready for service.

The mug, like her underwear, was borrowed. The breath, like the memory of her job, was fading. Thank god she was dying and unfit for work. Thank god no one would ever ask her about how early results could show up. Once she'd said, Start using the pills and drinking meal-replacement shakes, and if you're not completely satisfied, corporate will issue a full refund. No longer. The line of camels starts to decompose in the awful sun.

She was happy with the way things turned out. This was the fever. She remembered selling cookies for Girl Scouts, how her dad took the list to work, and how it came back filled out by his employees seeking promotions or bonuses.

He would make her deliver the orders to houses alone. They drove to the mall to pick them up, but business called him elsewhere. He took a box of cookies for the secretary. He was sleeping with the secretary, and Marjorie once walked in on them wrestling.

Back to dying, Marjorie stops feeling the blood's slow pull downward. The trickle of life escaping her leg. People are shopping all around her, unfazed, including you. Someone doused the burning kiosks and now the international mid-level marketing company, removing the small drained body, installs a new attendant, Marjorie's girlfriend Rebecca, who needs a second and third job to make ends meet.

Rebecca frowns disappointedly when transactions with potential clients (corporate jargon) don't end in sales. The stained ground of Marjorie's service trembles beneath her feet, temporary cease-fire.

Parade

WE ARE DOWNTOWN. THERE IS no celebration of Marjorie. The rich kids are hard to soothe, perpetually spoiled and hungry, unloved and angry. We are mad the company sent the worst car. A smudge on the windshield, half-tank of gas. Several friends have glowing recommendations for other homeless. We make a note to fire Leo. And we know Simon is trying his best, conducting traffic, but can't he see her coming first? This is our livelihood. We must see the parade or perish. Without this, we are nothing. We can't risk falling out of range of Marjorie. Every year, we toast Marjorie for her honor, courage, and civility in the face of defeat. She took on homelessness and won, losing her job, kitchen staff, and cars in the process. Her skills made her uniquely marketable. We saw the biopic. She stands for privilege and hard work. We are downtown for the same reasons. We hope she spots us from the motorcade, waves. If she doesn't, it could mean lights out. We could be anybody.

The paparazzi, poor freelancers looking homeless, snap photos for our social media. We have hundreds of thousands of followers. Because of Marjorie, we are innovators. We say this every morning on rising. We hear our neighbors bellow the same witness to Marjorie. We listen, all of us hollering before 4 a.m., confident ours is loudest. Her name is spilled across sides of buildings as a testament to sound decision-making, and we are secure in our finances. All of us drinking imported bottled water at the parade. We read Marjorie's new book, about the keys to success in every relationship, and this is the only book we will read again. We read it for the few next years, keeping its dog-eared pages close, memorizing passages. Marjorie is not on the jacket. It is a representation of Marjorie. Limited exposure creates brand awareness. The homeless work under us without benefits, and they are given the day off for the parade, but many choose to work. We aspire to a brand, like Marjorie. The homeless should be more dedicated to their families. The rich kids will learn one day, and their uniforms will gleam crisper than ever, smiles examples dentists show in after photos. They will be grateful.

We hate making small conversation with the driver amid screaming rich kids. The truth: We respect the suspense. Marjorie knows anticipation is paramount. The celebration, organized by politicians, isn't far from our buildings, but we hire drivers anyway, fearing everyone will show up in better cars. Several friends have debuted fashion lines this spring to rousing success. Several friends have rich kids in the best colleges. Several friends own high-end restaurants. We eat out occasionally because we know the owner. We are moments away from being homeless, wretched, and without. We vote in our best interest, because sponsored legislation doesn't let the homeless vote. We are upstanding and moral. Our votes count.

Everything hinges on the inner workings of the parade. Traffic is at a complete standstill: Simon failed to keep two walking homeless from crossing into the street, and now the city crew is cleaning up the horror. We are aggravated, and our shirt collars seem tight. We look unshaven. Here comes the parade. Down the block. We have to chase it on foot. We can see the back of the motorcade. We are running but the rich kids aren't coming. We will leave the rich kids, we threaten them. Look around you, we say, look at all the homeless people you don't know. The rich kids button up, trained in table etiquette from birth. They snap to attention like robot soldiers, running disjointedly, like something in them is broken but this makes up the distance in no time.

We are available to the poor for a price. Several friends have acquired shares for major networks. We strike exclusive deals with major networks. A prequel, tracing Marjorie's birth to present day, is in post-production, and we can't wait for the red carpet event hosted inside the gala, the exhibit ripped from her closets and garbage and sold to us for pennies. Some homeless, wishing for more, have probably gone—and we will dock their pay accordingly. Their families have gone missing, too, waiting at the end of the parade. We know because we read the lifestyle articles. Educated poor write lifestyle articles featuring homeless. These run on the back page. The homeless contribute free writing to major publishers, and we own the major publishers. Marjorie is a promise to the poor, but she is most like us.

We turn the corner, pushing through homeless friends and neighbors, but she's already gone: we can't see Marjorie. This year, it was rumored she would be wrapped in signature furs behind bulletproof glass. The rich kids hang their heads. The space between their legs is exploded by gloom. They have no life experience. I avert my eyes.

18C

Marjorie and Leo go apartment hunting in the Middle Ages. Property manager Simon busy with assassins, using gallows. The gallows stand fashionably alongside stiff, showroom furniture, in the middle of the open floor unit. Marjorie refuses to hold residence in squalor. Something about the outlets in awkward positions; they can't keep the royal couch. How the shower sputters cold, wimpy water. Simon can't quite follow. There is a microwave. If you don't rule, Simon knows, you don't rule.

While the reluctant couple bickers in the kitchenette like holy war, Simon tries not to listen. How can he spin the new crime statistics for good? Married by proxy, Marjorie and Leo amass more power every minute, counting dead relatives. Family won't often visit with encroaching armies . . .

Simon kisses the royals' feet in unit 18C, flogs himself at each showing. He lists off hot renovations, scheduled executions, but Leo wants peace on earth. The apartment brings isolation and dysentery to many people, but Simon shows the property anyway, losing shekels after the death of the one, true king.

"I decree: let the enemy dangle," says Marjorie, meaning law, trailing off after feeling the sick thunk of criminals dropping to the lobby, necks breaking in a row from Simon's rapid work. Disgusted, she swings a broadsword at the basic cupboard, brays at Leo as he crawls through fresh splinters. Why should she, a crowned royal, listen to this racket?

Wrestled from Marjorie, Leo will have the broadsword cast into useless crown jewels. He signs an executive decree at once, blasted over trumpet by an indentured messenger. Fitting a stowaway with a noose, freed from the destroyed cupboard, Simon almost groans. Catches himself. Examines the dead heretic in front of him. The body shows Marjorie ordered death by scaphism: ants and wasps lapping at voided milk and honey, others laying eggs inside an open mouth, ears, anus. Each traitor dies, an example reducing the threat, and Simon attends to the paranoid rulers every whim. It will take hours after his showing to wipe up this royal mess. Outside, and without shelter, weather torments the abandoned citizenry. They cower in the trees, once proud people locked in pagan celebration, converted to reluctant legal bodies. Marjorie and Leo try to destroy hangers-on with increasingly bizarre pronouncements. Distance from the problem keeps problems at a distance, to be handled later. The vacancy persists, and the vacancy persists, and the vacancy persists.

Marjorie Fishes the Monster Fish

THE TOWN ATE ONE MONSTER fish but that wasn't enough. There were ways to prepare the fish for cuisine that wouldn't kill you. The fish became the official export, a team mascot. Scale reproductions of the fish smashed across billboards, sandwiched into newspapers between articles about tragedy. Underground breeders gained fast popularity. If you didn't partake you weren't a patriot. Bankers and writers alike planned vacations for spawning season. It was a frenzy outside. Fish appeared in fountains, waterparks, aquariums—anywhere the cursed water system flowed. They adapted to scarce official food and shock treatments without fail. The monster fish overran lakes and rivers; pollution made them more cunning, voracious. There was high demand for their wares. Monster bones withstood cracking from sledgehammer heights, which made awesome dinner plates, useless art, sledgehammers, and people strung fist-sized scales from ends of necklaces for fashion, paying top dollar. People fucked using their eggs as lubricant. The fish were not breeding on their own. It was hard to tell. Marjorie was becoming tired of her job, but she did not want to go back to prison. Maybe they were born from disease or genetically modified, maybe they were alien life forms come to weaken humanity, but Marjorie didn't consider anything the true story. She never ate the thing out of respect for the lost.

The fish sometimes growled on land, skidded around and picked off children from unsuspecting mothers. A team of scientists, dead now, cited bony amplifiers for the noise. The scientists were executed for treason (they were trying to keep the species from propagating), but certain other parts confirmed this: proud horns on females, broken nubs on adolescent males, the sliver jutting from Marjorie's shin. Their size, which didn't stop growing, presented problems for transport, so the fish slowly adapted to land. Her line was cut and her pole was snapped: the river missile had caught Marjorie unaware. When it flopped on deck, she doubled over, ready to die. Marjorie was unafraid to die. Instead of attacking, the fish studied her for fishing it out of the river. Two red teeth poked stupidly out of its mouth. Hurt, Marjorie could describe the fish from memory. Its body oozed poisoned river so she wore gloves. Out of the water, its eyes looked wrecked. She remembered her brother Leo used to play like something had dragged him under the water: Then the monster fish was born, and the river swallowed up Leo for good. Her best friend Simon went shortly after that, thrashing on a school field trip to a neighboring village. The scales were like hard rock and took specific tools to puncture. Marjorie put her hand in its stomach, probing for Leo, Simon, traces of anyone. It came back empty, mangled by organ teeth but clinching guts, bits of used tires, and garbage.

Stomach acid was ruthless like memory. The motion was like a pickpocket. Her fingers were nimble, pawed everything cleanly, avoiding scabby meat. Marjorie got better at her job every day. She had two poles and she only brought one, so she wasn't out of luck. Families of monster fish bayed around her, shiny forms displaced among smokestacks. She lugged the full body of the monster fish to her truck, and grabbing the two dumb tusks, connected the pulley, hoisting the fish out of sight.

Marjorie Eats Our World

YOU APPEAR TO BE SWALLOWED. Marjorie doesn't chew our homes, she makes cud of our impossible life. Burps for room.

The grass is green, normally, but Marjorie flakes pink wax between crashing tree sounds, stomping gardens none of us will pick anymore, footprints cupping swamps of industrial skin. I hate you and Marjorie for butchering our life. I should've listened to Mom and ditched you at prom, but I swore you could change. How we met is a wonder, odds stacked against us, snobby in-laws and war tanks and unparting traffic. I remember we lived in the same dormitory and I knew you could be somebody, maybe, at least in student government. Instead: no one, all of a sudden, glued to the couch and stoned. Frenzied or dependent on drugs. The uppers. Disarming henchmen in your video game.

Now swollen Marjorie storms Arch Street, moaning between bites of gated communities. No no, I'm fine, but I wasn't fair to myself. I know your jiggly, milky-white center down to that embarrassing birthmark shaped like a fish, what you called a fading bruise our first time together.

I'm fine with the birthmark, but we were breaking up anyway, awake and in the middle of angry sex. Then it happened, the rashy hand of Marjorie plucked you up. Earlier, you mumbled Stop, this isn't working at all; talk nasty like a dirty bitch, but I pretended I didn't hear you: Some eighteen-wheeler spilled over on the freeway next to the house we were renting, doused vagrant Marjorie in toxic waste, sprouted her to planet-sized and starved. Immediately the neighborhood sounds ripped apart, as if an earthquake or a fire ignited.

I'm fine now, but I'm on the ground, still naked in bed, the bed intact, my leg twisted in pus. I'm going nowhere fast, but out there is Marjorie, giant, wreaking havoc on our world. She's eating our world. Okay, I'll be honest: You bankrupted us, bet unemployment checks on the Browns and lost, swearing This is their year after a 4-1 start. Stop believing you're sacred. Your sacrifice means nothing. Is it hard to breathe in that sticky mouth, the air throaty and bubbling with sores, plopped between teeth and rock-ing like a carnival ride?

Marjorie's mouth grinds through safer and safer neighborhoods, but I'll say it before you get too far away—her satisfied grunts ruin everything, but I'm glad you were swallowed, sorted by Mar-jorie's colossal sweating hands.

MurderLand

THE IV DRIP IS AN ocean rolling through you. There is nothing wrong with oceans under your skin. There's nothing wrong with the way the waves shock you, throwing weight into disappearing cold. There's nothing wrong with the way oceans move, guided by wind and parting and crashing, tasting unclean. Even your sister hates you afterwards: "Marjorie's a ghost," Rebecca says, picking at her nails accusingly. She switches the channel to something easy like Growing Pains, avoiding the news. But Simon isn't dead: See EMTs get sliced from head to toe. See cops as intestines, fat loosed, but no one ever listens to you.

At the beach party, your head was spinning drunk but you stumbled to the car, and there was Leo. He was still handsome beneath the charring, but the air smelled beefy. Watch blood skip down his beautiful face: The knife was stabbed into his ear like an ugly wave. Drowning is one of those things, Marjorie, like how a murder works itself into the recess of memory and festers there, and filmy it bores deeper and deeper and latches on to the greyest parts, and still you can't see past the throng of teenage bodies running for dear life. The dash clock blares three a.m., and this is way past curfew, but there is psycho redneck Simon cutting through victims with his steely machete. This is not a dream, Marjorie. You are living out the sequel of your nightmare; his mad eyes catch the same orange as the housefire. When the freak called Gables finds the hospital, you aren't surprised, just tired of fighting.

The doctors say trauma can be eased with medicine, but Simon is everywhere. He is in every word. A nature documentary: the shark breeches water, snatches the seal and drags it into the depths. A vegan, you always picked around meat, cautious of killers, but your mind is a different place after the investigation. You order plates of pork chops and greasy pizza from the cafeteria. Seconds on pudding, requests for fish. You don't remember not loving meat, ribs and Cornish hens and sausage links and, yes, scrambled eggs. The doctors are encouraged; your mind seems sharper, honest. Rebecca says, "Now you seem wild, out to sea." You are sixteen and smiling, and Rebecca is almost afraid of you. Dig in your heels, final girl: The open car yields access to the

Bowie knife. The people you love are dying over and over on a loop. When the freakshow called Gables loses track of you, an army of light, bring this knife down, rotate and push the knife blade into his soft chest. See every bleeding thing there.

Marjorie the Hand

OUR DEATHS WERE NEVER EFFICIENT ceremonies. The walls here were slick with power, and we couldn't lean comfortably against them. We were trapped inside a labor camp afraid of our memory, stalled amidst a hunger strike. Our swords were rubbish from that range: For months, steely cannons cut though our torsos like wet clay. Outside, the rebellion dawdled on, untrained and hopelessly outnumbered.

In the kitchen, Leo's tired mouth frothed unstoppably. As many dogs as kennels. Another joke. Leo told the same three jokes, a shadow of his former self. He was a soldier who kept us measured during reserves, until we were called up and the real horror started.

In the labor camp, we awaited the butt of the nephew's rifle like theater. Wards of the Hand, we were hated here but imprisoned anyway, a looming threat to Marjorie's order. We were soldiers once, recruited by the Hand, now fighting for the resistance and lined up in feeding booths. They fed us poorly.

Leo sucked nervous wind through one hole instead of two, ready to deliver again, louder each time. The Hand used torture. Even though I couldn't imagine torture, hungry, I imagined Leo tortured into silence, clamps and car batteries and caught on film. I hated Leo now, the loud mouth in camp. In these fantasies, something my degenerate uncle said surfaced: It's important to keep track of every possible outcome on the inside. I knew what was coming. I begged Leo to shut it, pleading sternly for reason. Leo was more or less spineless in the face of dinner.

Marjorie silenced the last cook who couldn't feed us. Because of this, we knew the hunger strike was working.

Now the nephew played chef. In the kitchen, the nephew was quiet but boiled water hissed over his cauldron. I checked once to see if the nephew had heard Leo's insane babbling. The nephew, a sentry guard before his swift promotion, had swung the butt of his rifle convincingly before. I remembered this, but next to me,

Leo cracked another stinker, asked how many Marjories it took to change out a light bulb. The same joke. I stayed stone-faced. We couldn't laugh at Leo, making jokes in his booth, afraid of how many lashes this netted us. Humor didn't offer respite from realized torture.

My stomach crooned. Of course we wanted to strike out but we were curled forever into ourselves, into our fear. Together we vied for the slightest position, chained to our booths. The nephew sang terribly in the kitchen, a jabbering nutcase slaving over gruel instead of war. We yelled madly during our hunger strike, defeated in every way but one. We splattered the wall with gruel, gray paste clumping on porcelain tiles.

I didn't trust the nephew as far as I could throw his meals: his Hand insignia was tattooed above the wrist, indicating a lifelong devotee. In the labor camp, the nephew played nice but still I resisted. I didn't eat anything the nephew cooked on principle, suspecting poison for my crimes. In the labor camp, there was gruel I could eat, but I didn't eat it. In the labor camp, we were fertilizer, feeding nothing planty, hardly an ideal. It had been so long since The Hand had pressed our rebellion into a ball for easy, compact storage. We were at the labor camp, being force-fed gruel, and because it was wartime, Marjorie the Hand was bored of executions but at least we weren't dead.

Death by Genius

ASK ANYONE, IT WAS THE children-gangs who changed the course of history. Unhuman agents of destruction, weaponized by grief, we watched them slice through Leo, parental locks, little SEAL teams on the footage. Wheezing contradictions: proudly dying of our problems, but we wished relief for their generation. New clean air to breathe. Minutes and Professor Leo's unsealed quarters were ripped open with rifle fire. We weren't interested in failed potions, old trophies. Later, cleaning up after the kids, we dreamed of different pastas, or what we'd steal for dinner, scrubbing circles inside those tall homicides.

Filthy shopping bags flapped in plain view on our world. Our husbands chased their women around kitchen islands, prescription erections flapping like hanged sheets. As children-gangs stormed our houses, waving assault rifles, we were speechless with virus rot. What did it matter anyway, to die there in our houses, choking on dictionary amnesia. But the children-gangs stopped us in our thoughts. They said, Find the patient zero for us and your lives will be spared. We slobbered virus blessings, hugging our tumored chests. We memorialized our suicided neighbors with ugly effigies, bulky statues on our lawns lit up and glowing.

It's unconfirmed, but Leo was gentle, if cursed to die like us. This is how his plaque reads at the foot of his statue. The radio of the universe was in flames, but Leo wouldn't stop trying to find a cure. While Leo blended potions in the kitchen, our ears were stopped with good virus wax. We didn't hate the sickness, really. We have good virus eyes, spotted with lesions, inside of good virus skulls. But this news came out. Blared TRAITOR into smartphones, robopets. We had to hitch home from the horror conference, tear down life in search of Marjorie inside our walls. Called her patient zero. Words plunged like drugs from needles.

We spent years lost, hiking alone through miles of uncombed forests.

Little changed after interrogations. We tried parts of Marjorie, different vials. Found her in the attic, curled between touching slats, open to the ruined world and willing. Bit our lips, licking good virus blood. Buried in the flowerbed, Marjorie's song thrummed the trees alive. A plane crash-landed in the city and everyone died on impact. The forecast called for rain, but the sun was out. It was winter then. The virus had slowpoked its way through humanity. Our radios disconnected from fortune. A dog shook violently in the unused schoolyard, chained to a nearby protest. Leo's rebels were exposed as our high-powered lights checked and rechecked for survivors, but the good virus had erased residual hurt. We washed the damaged bodies of dissent from our street. The fumes there were toxic but slow working. Marjorie tumbled out where we found her, chest cinching with stomach acid. But we forgot the exposed Marjorie instantly because our limbic functions had eroded. Suds pooled together then shrank away into wet nothing.

The sky was wide and cold when we threw ourselves off the bridge.

Once a Scorned Actor, Always a Horse

THE WAR HORSE'S VOICE IS a little girl's. A slight lilt to the emphatic song of pain, almost slurred, and reminiscent of her brothers before puberty. The horse stays masked in shadows and rolling in shit inside the single, rundown stable. Marjorie can hear the moaning horse clearly on her approach from fifty yards away. The stable is the only structure left standing for miles. She sneaks through the tall grass, stopping in increments to listen for the dangerous horde. Marjorie checks the exposed sky sinking above her, a drunk fog creeping along the horizon. A rough, wet missile. Now Marjorie crouches behind the dunes. Maybe whatever evil stalks this region has moved into hiding for the night. Marjorie progresses, tasting shelter, a happy caterpillar snaking noiselessly toward the source of somber life. The horse sighs when she opens the splintered gate, defeated. Enormous turds decorate the untamed straw of inconsistent care. The horse is a miserable sight, ribs all poked out from hunger. An anguished sun shines through infinite cloud cover and warms Marjorie's shoulders. Her mind is delirious from running. She should have worn a tough farm coat, hates the mild temperatures summoned by hard labor. The talking war horse is basically incontinent. The smell is what Marjorie prepared to face, but the actual vision causes to her to involuntarily gag. Amid the putrid burn of bile, she hears the scorned horse's cry again, drinks it down. It was the whispers that carried her here, away from the horrors of pulsing graves, half-dead shopkeepers closed early in the carnage, their stocks depleted and raided by monsters, now rations, too many eyes wormed out of their natural holes, parts kicked around heaps of people. Everything slicked in blood and alien fluid.

"Are you the director?"

Marjorie tenses, confused by the cadence of tea parties and make-believe.

"I asked, are you the director? I'm not interested in games."

"Who?"

"I won't repeat myself." Thwap, thwap … the sound of an impatient tail flung high and low. Marjorie scratches her ear, irritated by the buzzing flies. One thing the monsters couldn't eradicate: shit and the pests who live there.

"It's Christmas. I hope you're done shopping."

Another stunned silence escapes Marjorie's cracked lips. New questions snap Marjorie out of her dazed function. "You're special."

"Whatever do you mean I'm special? I'm a horse."

"But you can talk."

"So I can talk."

"But how? How do you talk?" The faroff chitter of mindless mouths fighting over soft meat. The march continues.

"How do you walk and breathe? I don't have time for this. I'm waiting for the director." The horse draws out an emphysemic snort. "I reported when it says on the call sheet. I'm an actor. Where is the director?"

"Someone is here?"

"Of course he is. And I'm starving to death. Literally. Go find him. Fast. Before I can't remember my lines. He's finished when I tell the union about this."

"But you're a horse."

"And you're a halfwit."

"But a horse can't talk."

"Name one that can drive. And tell them to fetch the car."

"I need to think."

The wind hoots softly against the unhinged door. Marjorie notices the time lapsed and composes herself. "I can't stay here."

"Did you expect a palace?"

"Stop talking to me."

"You're a joke. Stay in character."

Marjorie's stomach lurches forward, spins along with her head, as she feels the weight of her predicament. Her gnarled hands slide deeper into the muck of the stable, shit caked around her busted nose in splatters. Colder ground seeping between her scarred fingers. And the horse, professionally sedentary, makes no important flinch away from the clumsy fall. The halo of light from the stable now appears to Marjorie as an electric sign blinking Vacancy, Vacancy, Vacancy. Still, this roof is the only shelter before Marjorie's impossible journey to the next marker, what she read in the secret letter tucked away in her cheap puffer coat, a trek made more bizarre through hundreds of miles of alien spores, hybrid flora from distant stars wet with monsters. What used to be the city where she was raised. Memories threaten to eat Marjorie from inside out. Marjorie makes to sit against the fence, and the horse stays chillingly hushed. She can't sleep in this stinking hovel long. The winds gush apocalyptic reminders, screams of terrible planets locked in constant pursuit. They are at an impasse, an odd couple perplexed by odder circumstances. Persistent spirits despite dwindling health and scarcer daylight. Locked in contemplation, Marjorie starts to slip away from the world, coma-like, her heart encased in a stencil of the human form, worn away from unfair trials and rotten luck. There are the remnants of a dream forming in her nearsighted vision when the horse speaks up.

"You can cut me open. Inside, I am warm, and the cold won't diminish by wishing it gone."

This offer beats Marjorie awake in the wild shelter. "Say that again."

"I am large like a house."

"You don't mean that."

"Did you read the script? I am your only hope. There is a knife hanging on the wall above me. It is rusted but efficient. The jockey killed his wife with it when the war started."

Marjorie doesn't move, shivers.

"Do I have to spell it out for you? He feared living in this upside-down world, more than you or me, and set fire to the house after swallowing too much Ambien. The smell of burning flesh is perfectly horrid. Do it, babyface, slit my gassy, distended belly and live nicely for a spell."

"I can't."

"Come now. If you were a horse I'd've gutted you the moment I saw you idling in this stable. I wonder what keeps those things confined to the cities. Maybe I should draw them out with a whinny."

"No! Please!" Marjorie was burning with fever from the ears down. Thoughts of gnashing teeth and acrid spit; this couldn't be her end. As the gods from on high ripped humanity limb from limb, unceasing menace no one had accounted for. Amid their constant haggling and backsliding, peopled or not, no one saw this threat coming for the world. Just as she reasoned now, straining for the knife, one elbow scraping on the fence of the stable, her body wracked and struggling, minutes from the rashest decision of her life. She would listen to the talking horse. The wind sputters like a ghost, trees felled atop rickety swing sets and subsidized housing communities. The echo of progress gallops through the spaces of horrible deaths. That's when the war horse zooms up from the ground and bites into Marjorie's flank. The old horse finishes its scene with a lethargic, fleshy wail.

Wet Dream Date Night

THERE WAS A COIN ALREADY in the overlooked spring, and Simon picked it out. Explorers found the spring but did not always find a coin. Simon passed the coin through his scurvied fingers, tasting survival the way armadillos fling themselves at designer grilles. Explorers dedicated their lives to this journey, but Simon was different, eyes always drifting out of his sockets, into the feckless soup of conversation, ears scalded with obligation. His face changed in the bay, heavy mustache sagging from his sunworn lip like a worm, crusts of dried sunscreen streaked across his flat nose. He made the quest in ten months. In five years, legend had it, the same wish would come true for others. But Leo planned for absolution.

Though explorers lived a short life on estimate, succumbing to spraytanned cannibals, Stockholm Syndrome, and seasonal depression, a number of unrecorded wishes had occurred. Dogs, for example, always leashed to their masters, wished for chew things. Explorers often wished for more adventures, underwhelmed by the spring. Exes wished for new custody hearings, pending arbitration. Simon read hundreds of thousands of accounts in his university library. He arrived at the overlooked spring on a Monday, his socks wet with brine, ship sunk in the overlooked bay. Maybe he wished for a new ship. He fought through thick overgrowth of stinking rot and lazy rivers drowned with hair into the weekend, then he overslept.

Missing children guarded the spring, lost forever to parents, day care administrators. Say thank you, said the screaming, feral children. Thank you, said Simon, ready to pitch his wished coin. Then the facepainted children, singing murder ballads, shoved hatefully at Simon, almost knocking him down into the crosswalk. Simon pictured cracking his skull and drowning unfulfilled. The skylight licked Simon's shaved head with heat on the pavement. He was inside a waterpark. He bit his tongue, scarred by black licorice, and tossed the coin in, sealing his bond. He returned, shipless, to the overlooked bay, the sounds of depression loosed on his tongue. The cannibals were shouting from another expedition, roasting limbs of degenerate colleagues. The waterpark resumed crowd interference. The signs kept reading inversely for rest-stop bathrooms. What Simon thought was the overlooked spring washing newborns and lovers in light became a mall fountain sick with indigestion and skin flakes. This explained the bubbles.

Abscission

WE STOPPED SPEAKING. FORGET EVERYONE was glad. Forget everyone laughs at the bad parts and goes home confused. Forget our children were forever at war or perpetually miscarried. Never mind the dancing parties and burning old relics in a spiritual fire. Together we could raise new gods in safety and sustainability. But no one listens to reason or hope. Never mind the constant scrutiny, our neighbors trimming shrubs into impossible shapes. Our neighbors gloating unconvincingly, as if war stops after surrender. Talk about stock prices. Pretend to understand stock prices. Forget nonbelievers barred followers from organizing, locked her temples and demolished her holy sites. Forget the great wall sagged inward. Forget how it collapsed with the smallest push from the other side. Together we nervously bargained with our futures. Never mind the necessary killings. Our garden shears speckled with stranger blood. Forget we lost ambition defending our town. Waves of rebels were relentless but irregular. Talk about the end times. Talk about the stampedes of underworld fauna. Dream skeletal frames wielding swords. Go back to work. Believe in this world. Forget how subterranean plants screamed birdsong at us on our daily commutes. Forget the pounding on the windows. Leave the idea of worship in the dust. Forget the world upended into hell and how work was the only safe haven. Never mind the malware wreaking havoc on Technical Support. Drink the Kool-Aid and forget the old ways. Walk home, stepping around animated corpses, raised by the foolish necromancers. Forget how our infrastructure began to crumble, how the ground opened up and swallowed nuclear families, the lost pets they loved. Leave town council meetings encouraged but enraged. Forget ideas to rescue our town had dwindled. Forget how Marjorie still talked from underground. Forget we heard her looming voice like a sickness, whispered in gales from a mighty storm cell. Share how we lost sleep. Commiserate how we lost sleep covering our ears. Talk about survival. Talk about ways to appease the voices, what they were asking us for. Forget limits, sensibility. Dream about our bloodied hands, losing days or weeks on waking. Return to work. Days feel numbered. Then:

work stomped to bits and blooming fire. Pretend this is enough. Feel our souls descend through our toes like heart attacks. There are old gods the world stopped sacrificing for. Forget where we buried the goddess Marjorie in the dirt outside of town. Forget her sharp fingers, now tangles of fallen leaves and branches impeding the progress of travelers. She became a tree neglected by water. Talk about pilgrimage to the tree. Enlist elders to remember the way back to her burial grounds. Try and fail to escape the town by car. Forget the health of the goddess waned from our tiny deaths in traffic. Forget Marjorie was the goddess of revolution, noncorporeal and hungry for sacrifice. Forget we found nuclear shelters and met in secret to discuss further retreat. We moved underground and heard the voices even clearer. Yet the pounding came steadily from aboveground. Train ourselves to listen through the shouts of heresy and scripture. Heavy fists from nonbelievers coaxing us out for automatic lickings. Taunting us with words about divinity. Purpose. Listen in those shelters to the brazen lies adapted from outside of the great wall. Forget our heads swelled. Forget our hearts buzzed with civic suicide. The purpose moved like poison in our veins. Forget our shelters filled with reinvigorated bellows. Ignore our yellowy teeth. Ignore how our breaths smelled from rationing toothpaste for meals. Forget we pulled each other up by the shoulders, off our purple, scaly hands, and breathed out deeply. Feel the heavy armor made of garbage on our shoulders. Forget we were free, but we had sat on our hands. Hate the heavy armor for our clumsy hands and the cumbersome assembly. Welds cut into the dinner tables, into shag fibers of our shelters. Forget we were smitten with our goddess. Forget we knew oppressive reign and it was easy to return. Forget passing unserviced cars crashed into barricades along our pilgrimage. Leave under the pregnant fog of dawn. Vote to send children into foreboding dark buildings, use their smooth hands and weak voices to open doors. Never see the children again. Find other ways around the debris, into abandoned farms with stores of grain and meat. Struggle with progress in the rain. Forget our numbers were small, but capable, and forget we raised Marjorie into a homunculus in the cover of night. At the base of the tree we wept. We saw our murderous goddess resurrected. Forget we kept the homunculus Marjorie well-guarded. Move the homunculus around family to family for the new beginning. Forget assassins failed to carry out contracts on our vessels for the lord Marjorie. Forget we left hateful visitors with new scripts pierced artfully into their bellies. Hang the corpses from the street lights, first for warnings, then routinely out of boredom. Look at the letters and pretend we could scry the future. Interpret the signs from failing crops, worsening weather. Forget we built another wall to keep new survivors out. And a wall in front of that wall.

Forget how we sweat. Forget we needed to believe, and that it's important to believe in something if we're doomed to repeat it.

Acknowledgements

Thank you Jesi Buell, for the amazing opportunity and cosmic horror of printing a book for public consumption.

Thank you Mom and Dad, who still don't know how I will make any money. I love you both and will call soon. Thank you Brother and Sister, for saying nice things, like how proud of me you are, in person.

Thank you Matthew Gavin Frank, Orrin Grey, Lindsay Hunter, Anne Valente, James Brubaker, Amy Hempel, Michael Czyzniejewski, Mike Kleine, and Steven Dunn for reading and commenting on my work, many of you more than once. Thank you Daniel Williams for your inimitable illustrations. Thank you *Mikrokosmos and mojo literary journal* of Wichita, Kansas. Your group provided the catalyst that was confidence to send the manuscript around to publishers. I am overjoyed to see the literary programming grow in your community.

Thank you Driptorch readers.

Thank you Ore Dock Brewing Company and Bards & Brews. Thank you Jennifer A. Howard, for the unrestrained freedom to summon Marjorie. Thank you Northern Michigan University, for keeping me fed.

Thank you *Heavy Feather* disciples Bill Lessard, Hillary Leftwich, Kailey Alyssa, Hayli M. Cox, and Ryan Bollenbach.

Thank you Ohio family and friends, and those who encouraged me along this foolhardy journey. You know who you are.

Publication Credits

"Death by Genius" and "Abscission" appeared in *3:AM Magazine*. "Inedible Human Food" was selected by Amy Hempel as second place winner of *Mikrokosmos and mojo literary jorunal*'s fiction contest. "Everyone to Blame" appeared in *X-R-A-Y Literary Magazine*. "The Other Side of the Mirror of Lies" appeared in *Moon City Review*. "Subdivision" appeared in *Deluge*. "MurderLand" appeared in *Black Candies: The Eighties*. "Expiration" and "Simon Conjures the Dead" appeared in *Occulum*. "Meat Debt," "Almost Human," and "Dumped by Marjorie" appeared in *Quarterly West*. "Exceptional Air" appeared in *Hobart*. "Parade" appeared in *Corium Magazine*. "The Condition of Marjorie's Feet" appeared in *Matter Press: The Journal of Compressed Creative Arts*. "Marjorie's in the Basement" and "Marjorie the Hand" appeared in *Big Muddy*. "Marjorie Fishes the Monster Fish" appeared in *Fluland*. "Service" appeared in *Lit.cat*. "Marjorie and the Mountain" appeared in *SmokeLong Quarterly*. "Marjorie Eats Our World" appeared in *Vestal Review*. "The Age of Death, An Account" appeared in *Knee-Jerk*.

About the Author

Jason Teal lives in Kansas and edits *Heavy Feather Review*. This is his first book.